Albert Whitman & Company
Morton Grove, Illinois

The Origami Master

Nathaniel Lachenmeyer   Illustrated by Aki Sogabe

Shima the Origami Master lived alone, high up in the mountains. He never had visitors. His origami kept him company.

One day, a warbler chose the tree in Shima's backyard for its nest. It flew back and forth, collecting twigs.

When the warbler was done for the day, it sat
on a branch and watched Shima doing origami. From
time to time, it sang: "Hoohokekyo . . . hoohokekyo."

That evening, after Shima went to bed, the warbler flew
in through the open doorway and alighted on his desk. It
began to fold a piece of paper the way it had seen Shima do.

The next morning, Shima discovered a new paper elephant on his desk. He picked it up and examined it closely. It was simpler and more beautiful than any of the ones he had made. Someone is playing a trick on me, he thought.

Shima threw his elephants away. He decided to make a dragon. In his opinion, his origami dragons were the best in the world.

In the morning, Shima found a magnificent new dragon on his desk. It looked like it was about to come to life and fly back to its lair.

Shima spent the day folding origami spiders. At dusk,
he left his best spider on his desk. Then, he hid in the hall.
He was determined to find out who was making the origami.

In the middle of the night, the warbler flew inside and began making an origami spider. Shima watched in amazement. He decided to try to catch the warbler and learn its secrets.

Just after sunrise, Shima hiked down the mountain to the city below.

He bought a large birdcage and a lock, and returned home.

That night, Shima hid under his desk. When the
warbler arrived, he caught it and put it in the cage.

The warbler cried and beat its wings against the cage, but it could not escape.

Shima brought the warbler his best origami paper.
He gathered nuts and berries for it to eat.

But the warbler just
stared sadly at the tree,
where its nest was waiting.

Shima stayed up all night, making every origami animal he could think of. The warbler did not look at any of them. Finally, as the sun rose in the sky, Shima fell asleep.

When Shima woke up, he found the cage door open and the warbler gone. The lock was lying next to the cage. Beside it was an origami key.

Shima ran outside. The warbler's nest was empty. It made Shima sad to think that he had scared the bird away. Then, he saw the warbler returning to the tree with a twig in its beak. He smiled when he heard its beautiful song: "Hoohokekyo . . . hoohokekyo."

Shima realized how much he would miss the warbler if it left. He sat down and began work on something new—an origami nest for the friend he had made and almost lost.

Make Your Own Origami Bird

Diagrammed by John Montroll

Here is an origami design you can try. With practice, you, too, can become an origami master like Shima and the warbler.

It is best to use special origami paper, which is square and lightweight, with a color or design on one side only.

You can also use lightweight paper such as wrapping paper that is white on one side and has a design or color on the other side. Measure and cut the paper so it is square—fifteen centimeters (or about 6 inches) on each side.

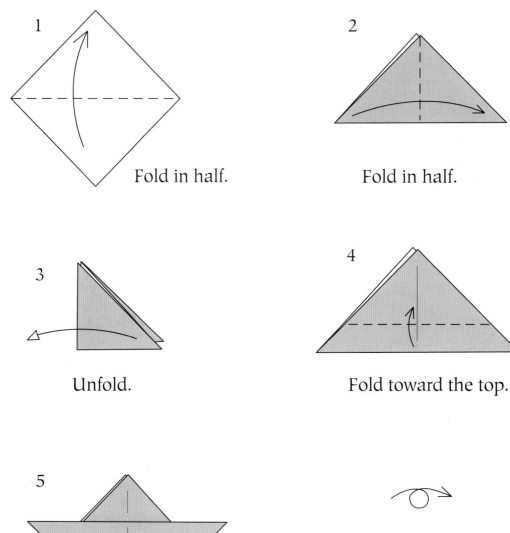

1 Fold in half.

2 Fold in half.

3 Unfold.

4 Fold toward the top.

5

Turn over.

6

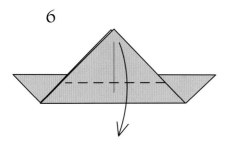

Fold one layer down.

7

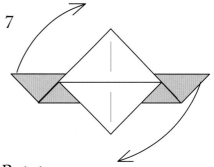

Rotate.

8

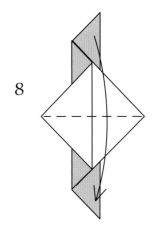

Fold in half.

9

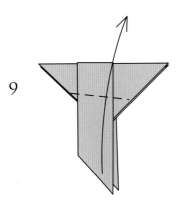

Fold the wing up,
repeat on the other side.

10

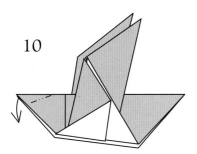

Fold the beak. Unfold.

11

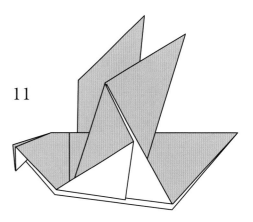

Invert beak on center fold.

You can find more origami designs by John Montroll in his books *Teach Yourself Origami* and *Origiami Sea Life*, published by Dover Publications.

*F*or Arlo and Nina, with love.—N.L.

*F*or Keaton and Kylie, from Baaba.—A.S.

Library of Congress Cataloging-in-Publication Data

Lachenmeyer, Nathaniel, 1969-
The Origami Master / by Nathaniel Lachenmeyer ; illustrated by Aki Sogabe.
p. cm.
Summary: An Origami Master whose only company has been his creations captures someone
who has been leaving him a magnificent origami animal each night.
ISBN 978-0-8075-6134-8
[1. Origami—Fiction. 2. Birds—Fiction.] I. Sogabe, Aki, ill. II. Title.
PZ7.L1335Ori 2008 [E—dc22 2008000140

The illustrations were created in cut paper and watercolor.
The design is by Carol Gildar.

For information about Albert Whitman & Company,
visit our web site at www.albertwhitman.com.